Murders
in the
Lonely
Graveyard

**Who's
Next?**

ELIZABETH UPTON

ISBN: 979-8-218-54611-3

Cover designer and interior designer: Deborah Perdue
https://illuminationgraphics.com

Published by

THE
Silver Woman
of Fire
PRESS

Santa Barbara, California 93105

Dedication

For all those who love and protect our planet earth

and its creatures large and small.

Also by Elizabeth Upton

Nonfiction

The Silver Woman of Fire

Secrets of a Nun

Exuberant Women Don't Age

The Mystery of Time Is Who You Are

The Mystic Swords of Love & Innocence

Fiction

The Shaman and the Mafia

At Home Among Sinners

The Web of Darkness and Light

Majic the Protector

Chapter 1

Sister Francis kneeled prayerfully before her mother's grave, moving her fingers prayerfully over her worn rosary beads. Autumn, her young grandniece, sat restlessly on the cold, stone bench with her, watching the yellow and black-striped butterflies skirt around the neglected tombstones. Yet she noticed how strangely the sun warmed each stone with light and grace.

"I dislike coming to Pillar Cemetery," complained Autumn. "It's so neglected and depressing. No one loves or cares for this place."

"My dear. The dead don't care," the old nun said. "I love it here only because this is the place where my mother is buried."

Autumn was not paying much attention to her grand aunt. Instead, she was watching a good-looking young man park his red Ferrari in front of her old Chevy, desperately in need of a paint job. She continued watching him as he strangely strolled around the tombstones, as if he were talking to the dead. Then, he started walking up the hill in their direction. *Please don't come here,* Autumn thought.

"Good morning. I'm Brien Hogan," he said to Autumn, extending his hand with a kind smile. He was indeed good-looking, dressed in tight blue jeans and a white polo shirt.

"Do you come here often?" asked the nun. "This is my first time. When I was a child, my mother used to take me to cemeteries and teach me to revere the dead who had lived in her words, Once upon a time."

"How wonderful," said the nun. "Today is the anniversary of my mother's death, and I've come here every year on this very day, though my grandniece, Autumn, finds it disturbing." She moved her fingers over another notch on her rosary beads. "She's always worried that a ghost might jump out at us," the nun chuckled.

"When we were driving into the cemetery, a truck nearly hit us. It passed us in such a hurry. There were two men in the back of the truck with blankets and sheets flapping all over," said Autumn.

"How disturbing," Brien said.

Sister Francis placed her attention once again on praying the rosary. Brien saw this at as an opportunity to converse with Autumn.

"Do you work around here?"

"I live in Sausalito. I'm a Realtor," she said.

"Here. Take my card. Maybe you know someone who may be interested?"

"Here's my card as well."

Sister Francis continued to pray, then looked at Autumn and motioned that they should go. "Good day, young man," the old nun said. Autumn nodded goodbye.

Sister Francis and her grandniece walked down the hill arm in arm to the car when the old nun realized that her rosary beads were missing.

"Oh my, Autumn. I've lost them," Sister Francis said. "Can you find them? Just look around, my dear."

Autumn rolled her eyes. "I need to get going, Auntie. I have appointments." But the good-natured young woman decided to spend a few minutes meandering through the tall grass and weeds in hopes of finding the rosary. Autumn was just about to walk back up the hill to the old stone bench when Sister Francis suddenly felt tired. She decided to drop her aunt at the convent, cancel her next appointment, then return to Pillar Cemetery to look for the rosary. It would be a quick trip down the road. Just five minutes.

When Autumn returned to the cemetery, she was alarmed by how drastically the scene had changed. There was a large police presence and yellow tape surrounding the dilapidated mausoleum near to where they had been sitting.

Brien, who had decided to explore the mausoleum after the two women left, had discovered two dead bodies wrapped in long rugs which covered their faces. He also heard a crying baby. He picked up the tiny infant, wiping the dirt from its mouth.

"Christ," he said to himself, as he reached for his cell phone in his coat jacket pocket to call the police. The infant was frantically crying, so he tucked the baby inside of his jacket to keep it warm.

As he waited for the police to arrive, he called Marietta, his older sister and a pediatrician, who made it her mission to care for abandoned babies until they could be placed in a safe home.

Upon seeing the police, Autumn wanted to leave, but she was trapped in. Too many police cars. As she watched the scene unfold, she could see Brien up on the hill talking to a police captain.

Marietta pulled into the cemetery. She abruptly stopped her car, left the door open, and ran toward her younger brother.

"I'll get the baby out of here before anyone tries to stop me," she whispered in Brien's ear. She took the baby from her brother, wrapped the child in a warm blanket then quickly hurried to her car. She gently placed the baby in a car seat and buckled the child in, turned on the ignition, did a tight U-turn, and sped away.

"Hey! Why is that woman taking off with the baby?" yelled the police captain to the other officers.

"Easy does it. Officer Whitecuff, is it?" Brien asked calmly, looking at the officer's badge.

George Whitecuff looked at Brien. "Who the hell are you? And how long have you been here?"

"I was the one who called the police," said Brien. "I was visiting the cemetery."

"Oh, really? Doing what?" Heat rolled up Brien's back, but he was determined to stay calm.

"I sometimes visit cemeteries."

"Hell! That's so weird."

Brien ignored the officer's insult. "I was exploring the mausoleum when I found those two bodies and immediately called the police," he said. "Here. Take my card. Get a hold of me if need be." Brien quickly turned around and walked away from the crime scene.

"Hey. Who the hell says you can leave?"

Brien wasn't worried. Not about the police captain's confrontation, but about the unfortunate pair he had just found. When the rugs were lifted, he saw their faces. It was a man and a woman, that looked Chinese. Brien hoped to God that they weren't Mr. and Mrs. Wong, his principal witnesses in the notorious Leo Mancini murder case. He knew that Mrs. Wong had a three-month-old baby girl now in the care of his sister. He hoped against hope that none of this was a coincidence. On the way to his car, Brien passed the broken-down tombstone where he had met the nun and Autumn, then noticed rosary beads lying beneath the bench. He picked up the beads. This would be a good opportunity to call Autumn, he thought, but he needed to get to the morgue before the police did. Autumn remained in her car. She had noticed Brien speeding from the cemetery. She picked up his business card, which she had placed on the dashboard and glanced at it. "Christ. He's Brien Hogan, the new lead prosecutor in the San Francisco District Attorney's office," she said to herself. Her best friend, Claire Hobbins, who was working for him as his assistant, had recently told her about him, and that he was great to work with but in some ways complicated.

Chapter 2

A black Ford police truck parked near Autumn's car was box-ing her in. She tensed when Chief Finn Begay quickly ap-proached her and asked her to lower her window. He was different in appearance from the other officers. He held his police cap in his hands, did not wear a jacket, just a black shirt with his badges displaying his five-star Chief of Police stripes, and did not carry a gun. Chief Begay was tall, at least 6'2", with jet black wavy hair, and from his short-sleeved shirt, she could tell buffed to the max, and, Christ, a real looker.

"Hold up," he commanded. Autumn's heart was pounding. "Don't leave."

She forced herself to look into his piercing, emerald eyes. "Give me your full name and how long you've been here."

"My name is Autumn Raven. I came here about a half hour ago with my aunt, who is a nun. We visit her mother's gravesite on this day every year."

"Was there anyone else here?"

"Just that man over there leaving in his Ferrari," she said pointing to the shiny, red sports car speeding away.

"When we got here, a driver in an old grey Dodge pickup nearly hit us," added Autumn.

"Anyone else in that car?"

"Two other men."

"What did they look like?"

"Both wore caps and dark sunglasses, impossible to describe."

"What did the pickup look like?"

"Rusty. Beat up. Dirty with rugs and towels flapping all over in back of the truck."

"Did you get the license plate?"

Trying to control her nerves, sensing that Begay knew who she was, she said, "LCH531 San Francisco."

"Thank you. You're free to go." He gave her a slight smile.

She was taken aback by his smile, which changed his entire persona from tough cop to a hot guy.

Begay watched her drive off, recalling everything he had read about Autumn Raven, a once rising-star detective who left the department one month before he had arrived. Under his watch she would have done well. He had no doubt she had been treated harshly and unfairly after reporting to the Chief that her supervisor had attempted to rape her in the women's shower. She had sent Stance to the E.R. with a concussion. That he flat-out lied she had attacked him with no provocation was outrageous. Unfortunately, no one had come to her defense. Everyone was intimidated by Stance, the assistant chief.

Chief Bradley of thirty years at the time had become seriously dysfunctional, ignoring police misconduct and many serious situations, and worse yet, befriending Mafia Barbieri, and often playing poker with him for Christ's sake. Begay had quickly fired Stance for a long list of grievous problems. He was impressed by the way Autumn had conducted herself and now was doing real estate. Good for her.

Autumn thought about her good friend Otis, when they attended the police academy together. Their friendship continued and she was often a welcome guest at his home, enjoying time with his wife and three-year-old girl. In a short amount of time, Otis had been recently promoted to police captain. Autumn was happy for him.

She recalled when she was assigned to the main police office with Otis. The stuffy room was filled with police officers busy at their desks. Sid, a troublemaker, shouted, "Hey look who's here, a black-faced nigger." The room grew stone quiet. Otis punched Sid in his face, knocking him flat on the floor slamming him back and forth.

"What the fuck did you call me?" he asked, hitting him again.

"Nothing. Nothing."

"Never again," yelled Otis. No one had come to Sid's defense. And that was a good thing.

All the police officers watched Sid crawl painfully out of the room. No one dared help him. The feeble chief came out of his office looking around. "What's going on?" he asked. Chief Bradley's phone rang, and he shuffled back in his office, shutting his door.

From that day forward, no one dared humiliate Otis, a handsome light-skinned man of Native American, Black and German heritage, who was often contacted to pose for sports magazines.

After Brien left, police Captain George Whitecuff went back to the mausoleum looking inside the door window and suddenly startled.

"Oh, Christ," uttered George. He motioned for Begay, who had just finished talking to Autumn, walking toward him to hurry up and meet him at the top of the hill.

Begay stopped a hundred feet from the mausoleum's door digging his shoes back and forth into the ground. He put on gloves and started feeling the marble. He smelled the front door, pulling back and running back to his patrol car on his phone.

"George, get everyone the fuck out of here. Drive your car a thousand feet away. Pull your windows up. Stay put until I get back to you."

Within minutes two fire engines arrived. Firemen wearing protective gear holding a steel pole hurried out. They tried opening the front door of the mausoleum to no avail, then rammed it open.

Fire Chief Randy half ran to Begay.

"Sir we have serious problems. There are two dead bodies in there. Young boys maybe nine, give or take, from what we can tell."

"My God," yelled Begay. "I need to see them."

"You must suit up. Everything is contaminated. The bodies have to be watered down, then wrapped from head to toe and taken to the Barkley Morgue."

Begay looked at the boys' bodies, shocked, and, for a moment unable to speak.

"Sorry," said Fire Chief Randy. "Do you know who they are?"

"Sadly, I do. I'll contact their mother."

Begay phoned Judge Manchester. "I need to see you."

She detected the emotion in the Chief's voice and put her hands to her face, sobbing. Begay turned his attention back to Fire Chief Randy.

"We're going to power wash everything down in the mausoleum and in the surrounding areas. It's too hazardous for anyone to go in or around there. We'll rope it off for twenty-four hours. I think it's wise if you put police protection around this cemetery given these terrible circumstances."

"Done, Chief," Begay said, whispering to himself. "I'll get the motherfuckers killing the Manchester boys. I swear to God." The boys were the sons of Judge Manchester and also good friends with his children. He pulled over to the side of the road fighting his rage.

Chapter 3

Brien parked a block from the city morgue where the bodies had been taken. He walked around the corner then ran up the rickety backstairs badly in need of repair, only to find a policeman at the entrance of the morgue. He waited until the officer walked down the long hallway to the restroom, hoping to God almighty that the victims were not the Wongs. He opened the door to the morgue where a young doctor was examining the murder victims' bodies.

"Sorry to interrupt, but I need to know if the victims on your table are Asian. Please."

The young doctor was shocked. "Who are you? No one is supposed to be in here."

"I work in the DA's office. A married couple by the name of Wong are my lead witnesses in a murder case. I know I am not supposed to be here. But I desperately need your help."

Brien watched the doctor pull back the sheet covering their bodies. "Take a look and get out of here as fast as you can. Run. Use that other back door," he said nervously.

"I understand," Brien said, bowing apologetically. Just as he headed out the back door, Brien heard the officer yell, "Hey. Everything all right?"

"Yes. No problem, sir." Once the officer went back to his post, Brien ran down the backstairs then drove home and parked in his four-car garage. His heart was bounding and he took a few deep breaths, trying to get a hold of himself. He was in shock. His fears were real. Mr. and Mrs. Wong, his star witnesses, had been murdered. His case had just gone down the toilet.

Brien composed himself and put his hand inside of his jacket pocket, pulling out the nun's rosary beads and Autumn's card. He dialed her number, and she picked up the phone. "Sorry to bother you," he said, "but I found your aunt's rosary beads at the gravesite you were vising. I'd like to return them to you."

"Thank God," said Autumn. "She's been so distraught."

"I can drop by or meet wherever you'd like?"

"Meet me at Danny's at six. I have a bunch of work stuff going on."

"Will do."

Brien took another deep breath. Just being with this sexy woman would ease his nerves. My God, did she say Danny's? Brien tried to pull himself together. First thing tomorrow morning he'd work with his assistant Claire Hobbins to put together a new action plan.

Begay had quickly arranged for Judge Manchester to be taken to the morgue in a private police sedan, and with twenty-four-hour protection including a personal bodyguard. He and his assistant chief, Ronald Rowling, went to the basement where darkness called itself home.

"Just found out those two boys recently reported missing are the twin sons of Judge Manchester," said Begay

Rowling distanced himself from him, feeling raging heat emanating from his body. He waited for a response for what felt like a hundred years. Finally, Begay began to speak quietly, a dangerous sign.

"I know Judge Manchester well, got to know her at our school parent meetings. My kids loved her boys. I often had them over for dinner." He paused. "We also have that fucking Mancini case and now the Wongs have been murdered."

"Do you think Mancini put a hit on the Wongs?"

"Hell yes."

"What about the children?"

"Mobs have an unwritten rule never to kill children."

"Who then?"

"It had to have been done by Mancini's son. Alonzo's a fucking nutcase," Begay continued.

"Officer Carey is going to be our lead investigator because he's the most successful detective we have on the force. I know he'll need help given his high-strung personality. He'll need food and rest. Officer Spenser will be a perfect fit. He's a foodie. He lost the 20 pounds that Carey needs to gain." Both men laughed, knowing that Carey and Spenser would make a perfect team.

When Carey had graduated from the police academy, his commanding office had contacted Begay.

"You need to know a few things about Carey," he had said. "He graduated with extremely low marks in every physical area, except for walking and running. I made an exception when I saw that he aced all of his written and case exams. Gotta confess there was a day when I was unable to find the combination to a very old safe stored with secret documents. Well, out of the blue I thought of Carey. In minutes, he opened the safe and gave me the combination. After that, I didn't give a rat's fuck. I passed him. The funny thing was when it came time for our police cadets to graduate, we had to bring in a skilled seamstress because he was so damn skinny and still is. Any questions?"

"I'm sure Officer Carey will work out just fine," said Begay. Such recollections were just what they needed to ease the tension.

"You know he hides his gun in his locker even though he knows how to use it," added Rowling.

"Yeah. In time that may change." Begay knew the police academy promoted Carey because he was a super brain and since had been able to solve murder cases more quickly than anyone he had worked with in his career. Whatever Casey needed in solving these notorious murders, my God he'd get it.

"Would you get my gun from my safe? Just don't want to go to my office just yet," said Begay, giving Rowling the combination.

Rowling removed Begay's Glock 22 with his initials, F.B. engraved in silver on its handle. It was obvious that Begay rarely wore it or used it. Now the die had been cast in blood, thought Rowling. He returned to the basement, putting the gun on the card table, watching Begay take it out of the leather case and strap it to his belt.

"It's horrific what's been happening to Judge Manchester," said Begay. "Her husband died three months ago from cancer, and now she's faced with the murders of her only children."

"Do you think Brien Hogan, the head prosecutor, and his assistant with the Mancini mob case need protection?" Rowling asked.

"If needed, I'll provide it. I'll brief my officers about this case. This is a fucking war I intend to win."

When Begay got back to his office, he spoke to Mayor Reynolds about the dreadful murders. "I know Judge Manchester personally. Her sweet young boys played with mine at St. Vincent's school. Mr. and Mrs. Wong the procurator's main witnesses were also murdered."

"My god." After a long pause, he said, "Whatever you want, Chief," broken up by what had transpired.

Chapter 4

Autumn back home ran her fingers through the thick coat of her adopted German Shepherd, Winston, licking her hand and a happy home for her three chickens, and an elderly duck refusing to die. Even though her contact with Brien Hogan had been brief she wanted to know more about him and went to her computer doing a search. He was age 33 and single, graduated from Stanford with a law degree from Harvard. Both of his parents are scientists living in Sierra Madre, California. His older brother is an orthopedic surgeon. His sister teaches physics at Berkley. What a remarkable brain wave family. She wondered where he lived but resisted the urge to find out.

Out of law school Brien worked in London as a procurator for the prestigious law firm of Stanly & Brady winning the well-known case of Barnes, a notorious criminal involved with murder for hire, including securities and insurance fraud.

She couldn't believe it. Brien had only been out of law school barely two years. That law firm had many seasoned successful attorneys. Why did they choose Brien with no experience to be their lead prosecutor? The judge, Glen Cleaver supposedly in good health at the time, suddenly died, cause of death unknown. She wondered if Brien knew anything about it and was determined to find out. She was convinced he was supposed to lose that case given his lack of experience, but why?

Needing to settle her nerves, Autumn went outside to play with Winston. *My God. I asked Brien to meet me at Danny's, a hot dancing and dinner club known for its sensational singers from all over the world. I must have been out of my mind.* She pulled out his business card and picked the phone. No answer. No address on the card. She would have to go to Danny's. She had to get her aunt's rosary beads. *Just go there and get them outside of Danny's. But he'll be dressed up waiting for me.*

Frantic, she called Bonnie, her young Irish neighbor.

"When was the last time you were at Danny's having a hell of good time?" Bonnie asked.

"I can't remember."

"'Well, make the best of it,' as my granny used to say. Lord, rest her soul. I'll come over and we'll look in your closet and see what we can find," Bonnie said, laughing.

Police Captain George Whitecuff had watched Begay speed off from Pillar Cemetery. The mausoleum had been roped off and a police detail put in place. He returned to his car recalling the day Begay became Chief. Begay had taken over the San Francisco Police Department in a dismal state, meeting with his officers in less than five days.

Two hundred and fifty police officers filed into the Brady room. Everyone had been given a folder with their name on it. Inside was a bio of Chief Finn Begay and his Deputy Police Chief, Ronald Rowling. It didn't take long for everyone to get a solid idea of whom they would be reporting to. Chief Begay had graduated at the top of his class at Texas A & M in International Studies. He also had an M.A. in Criminal Law.

After three years serving as an Army Ranger, and their top-grade sniper, Begay joined the police force in Houston, Texas, and soon became their Chief. He was married with children, a boy, nine, and a girl, seven. He also had a boy that died at the age of five from a sudden brain blood clot. His wife also attended Texas A & M, receiving an M.A. in Architectural Design when the two first met and soon got married.

Ronald Rowling, Deputy Police Chief, graduated from NYU with a law degree. He was a widower. His wife was with child and died when she perished in a fatal car accident. Two years later, his eldest brother, a fireman, was shot and killed in New York by a gang member, later convicted and serving a life sentence at Five Points Correctional Facility in New York State.

Rowling decided to return home to Houston and joined the police department where Begay was Chief at the time.

Whitecuff was surprised and worried after opening the envelope. Why in the hell would Begay's and Rowling's personal information be given to the officers? It didn't take them long to understand that they had overcome adversity. They were tough and the best of the best, both having advanced college degrees and life challenges. Begay's first speech to his police officers still gave Whitecuff the chills. Begay and Rowling were both tall, at 6'2", and walked with the stride of tough-ass soldiers. Anyone would be God dammed to mess with them. "By now, you know a bit about us," said Begay. "I've been hired by Mayor Reynolds of this fine city to be your Chief of Police and to clean up the decay in this police department." He paused. The heat in the room was mounting.

"Listen to me very, very carefully. I will not be your friend. I will not listen to your shit. I will not join you at bars. I will not sit with you at restaurants. I will not socialize with any of you at any time. Look at me. I may be young, but I've been around the block. Don't take anything I say or do for granted if you choose to remain in MY police department. In five months, give or take, you won't recognize this police department." Whitecuff remembered finding it hard to breathe at that moment. "I have established new rules to help you become not only outstanding police officers in San Francisco but the envy of every police department in the state of California. No more smoking in any police offices. Short smoke breaks are allowed outside and make it damn fast. This rule will save your lives. I don't want to hear any of your whining."

The tension in the room was skyrocketing. But Chief Begay was not finished. "Every officer, when inside the police buildings, except for the entrance, will put their guns in their lockers. No officers will be allowed to take home their guns except for those I deem to be outstanding in rank."

"Sadly, too many wives and children have been abused, and some killed. At this moment these horrific situations end, so help me God. You'll hate me but your wives and children will be grateful and live in peace and will thank God almighty that I have saved them."

"I've arranged counseling for all those who have suffered mental and physical abuse including a task force set up for their counseling and protection. All officers responsible for such egregious behavior will be fired, jailed, or put on probation." George Whitecuff could still feel the shock and unbelievable tension in the Brady room when Scott shouted, "Who gives you the fucking right?"

Man, oh man, that was one hell of a mistake. Begay pulled Scott out of his chair, his voice cracking like thunder. "I know about you, asshole, head of the Dragon gang, wearing dragon tattoos on your ankles, stealing, intimidating officers. Your wife is under protective care as I speak." Begay dragged Scott to the front of the room and punched him in his face.

"It gives me fucking pleasure to fire your ass," he said, waving to the officer at the door to cuff and drag Scott out. Begay waited a few minutes for the officers to recover. The air conditioner blew full throttle. Everyone hated Scott and every officer began stomping their feet with approval. For a few minutes, Begay had everyone stand up to release the tension.

"Please sit," Begay said, returning to business. "Inside your folders are lists of officers to be fired, lists of officers who may choose to retire, lists of officers that will be given notice to improve, and a list of outstanding officers to receive promotions. Anyone with a snake tattoo will have it removed immediately. I am providing help to have this done at no cost. Anyone who wants to keep them will be fired." *But, hell, Chief Begay still wasn't done.*

"I don't want my department to be a bunch of nitwits. I want everyone to get their A.A degree and if you want a B.A. this will be provided at no cost thanks to the generosity of Mayor Reynolds. If this is something you don't want to do, you will be required to take

60 hours of updated information at the police academy, on every aspect of fighting crime, as it relates to your police officer rank. You will be offered assistance to achieve these goals."

Everyone began clapping when Begay finally smiled, which amazingly transformed him like a come to Jesus meeting.

Now it was Chief Rowling's turn to take the mike. "All of you have been given a white envelope. Please open it. "Inside were annual sports tickets for basketball and football games and a small paper with Rowling's private phone number, stating, *I am available 24 / 7.*

For a few brief seconds, the officers were stunned then started yelling and clapping. Shivers went up Whitecuff's spine, savoring that moment. The message sent was clear: Chief Begay was the bulldog and Rowling was the dove, both necessary for the rehabilitation of the police department.

Before Begay took charge it was routine for many officers not to show up for work, or file their reports on time, or attend training sessions and much more because of the disfunction of the old police chief too often out of it.

Whitecuff felt proud of himself. He dropped out of college but had since received his B.A. degree in American Studies. In a short time, the San Francisco Police Department had become the envy of every police department in California with a growing list of police wanting to work for Begay.

Scott sued the police department and lost. His wife quickly divorced him. He was arrested for robbing a bank and sent to Pelican Bay State Prison. Officer Whitecuff was later promoted to rank of captain.

Chapter 5

When Brien arrived at his French country home on two acres five miles past Sausalito, Leonardo his house manager and chef greeted him in the kitchen. He had retired from owning restaurants in Los Angeles and lived next door to him in a small Tudor house.

"Interested in dinner?" he asked.

"Nope. Going out tonight at Danny's."

"Fantastic. That's quite the place. Going with any one special?"

"It's a first time get together."

"Lucky girl," remarked Leonardo. He was enjoying his retirement and, when asked, he offered Brien fatherly-type advice.

Brien entered his office, shutting his door and feeling distraught about the deaths of the Wongs. He was determined to get a grip. After an hour or so, he spoke to Claire Hobbins, his legal assistant. "Wonder if you can come down here tomorrow noon? I have terrible news. The Wongs have been murdered. Their bodies were found at Pillar Cemetery."

"Holy Mother of God," she said. Brien could hear her slamming something. "See you tomorrow."

He made the decision not to tell her that he was the one who had found the murdered Wongs, and that their baby was now in the care of their grandparents.

Brien had chosen Claire Hobbins to be his assistant, feeling she was best of the thirteen attorneys in in the prosecutor's office. He liked her background: a USC law degree and years of experience working in the San Francisco office for the past three years. She was married with three children. Her husband owned a paint shop. She was perfect, talented, and hard-working with a wonderful sense of humor.

No matter how depressing these murders were, Brien felt it wasn't the end of the world and hurried into the shower, preparing for an evening at Danny's with Autumn.

"Danny's?" he shouted aloud. *Unbelievable.*

"I lost my mind telling Brien to meet me at Danny's," Autumn said to Bonnie.

"Worry not, meant to be, saith angels from above. Calm down, darling," Bonnie said. "Take a deep breath. I'll help you with your makeup. Make you look hot and sexy." Bonnie emigrated from Ireland seven years ago and now owned her own salon. She was a good friend to Autumn. "That's the last thing I want to be," said Autumn.

"Easy does it. With all those people milling around, no one will notice you," Bonnie said winking. Autumn was drop-dead beautiful with mouth-dropping curves. Folks would be half-dead not to notice her.

"Come on, lassie," Bonnie continued. "Frowning doesn't become you. You don't need much work with that beautiful hair of yours."

Bonnie pulled out a short, bright red dress designed to show off Autumn's sensual body.

"God. No. That dress is insane. That's why I hide it in the back of my closet. Toss it in the trash. Please."

"I can't do that. You're running late," Bonnie quipped, pulling the dress over Autumn in a motherly fashion.

"I don't know what to tell him," Autumn complained. "Tell him the truth. Where you intended to meet him. Trust me, he won't give a diddly."

"This isn't a date. I just want to get my aunt's rosary beads."

"Relax pretty girl. You've been working like a dog. No offense, Winston," Bonnie laughed, patting the German Shepherd affectionally.

Autumn walked to Danny's, a short distance from her house. People were waiting in a line at least two blocks long. She saw Brien standing near the door, smiling and waving at her. The two were immediately escorted inside. He had to force himself to stop staring at her.

"Sorry about telling you to come here," Autumn apologized. "I was frazzled over my aunt's loss of her rosary beads. It was supposed to be at Joe's down the street, instead of Danny's nightclub, for God's sake."

"A good mistake because Bon Jovi's band is going to be here just for this evening. That's why crowds of people have been waiting to get in."

"How did you get us in so quickly?"

"I went to school with the Josh Cummings, the manager. I've come here on occasion. Most of my family lives in the Bay area."

Their waiter led them to a side table, offering a shade of privacy but to no avail with everyone staring at the handsome couple. Autumn tried to pull down her short dress before she sat down.

"Here, take your aunt's rosary beads. I don't want to forget to give them to you. Wine perhaps? Tea. Coffee. Nuts. Creepy crawlers?"

She laughed. "I would enjoy a glass of wine."

"Zinfandel?"

"My favorite." Autumn had intended to sip just one glass of wine very slowly.

"I have a feeling you know more about me by now than I know about you," he said chuckling.

"How would you know that?"

"I was brought up with two sisters. Often a matter of survival since I was the youngest and only boy. I knew what they were up to most of the time," he said grinning. It took Brien enormous effort to remain a restrained gentleman.

She wanted to ask him about the trial he won in London and about Glen Cleaver the judge who died suddenly and why he had been chosen to be the head prosecutor. But that would wait for another time. Their meal was served quickly.

"How was your afternoon?" she asked.

"Busy needing to care for delayed reports left for the weekend," he said, leaving out the news of the murders. "How's your real estate business coming along?"

"Fine," she said. A small lie.

She had cautioned herself to sip her wine slower but that didn't happen. Bon Jovi had joined his band. Everyone was going wild and clapping when he started singing, "Living on a Prayer." During the break, the DJ played dance music.

"Would you enjoy dancing?" Brien asked, reaching for Autumn's hand.

"Of course," she said, unaware that many eyes had been fastened on them. Brien led her to the far corner of the dance floor as the music grew sensual. Autumn allowed herself to lean into his chest feeling his heartbeat. With enormous effort he controlled himself from kissing her at all.

At the end of the evening, Brien drove Autumn to her cottage and walked her to the front door. "I've had a wonderful evening," he said. "I want to be with you again."

"That would be nice," she said. He caught her swaying unsteadily.

"I'll take you inside and put you on your bed," Brien said, "but you must tell your dog to be kind to me."

"I can do that." Autumn gave Winston a command. He backed away but lifted his lip in warning.

Brien helped Autumn into her bed, putting a blanket over her. He wanted to hold her sensual body and make love to her. In seconds, she was sound asleep. He backed to the front door as Winston gave a threatening growl. He planned to contact her tomorrow morning. He wanted her in his life more than he had ever wanted any woman.

Chapter 6

Next morning Autumn met with her friend Claire for their early Saturday morning walk around Sausalito. She thought better about not telling her about her evening with Brien at Danny's. "Gotta say I've been so curious about Brien winning that notorious white water crime case in London. Do you know anything about it?" Claire stopped, beginning to wipe her eyes.

"I don't know if I possibly can."

"Honey why not. What's going on?"

"Let's find a bench."

"Maybe it's about time I finally told someone what happened," she said, pushing herself up straighter in the bench. "Just like you, I wanted to know why Brien of all people was chosen to be the lead procurator in that notorious Barens case only two years out of Oxford law school for Christ's sake, and with no experience.

"One afternoon after we had finished our work, I asked him why he had been so chosen. He went ballistic, hollering at me never to bring it up again, slamming his fist on the table. I ran downstairs to an empty cafeteria crying uncontrollably."

"My God."

Claire finally calmed down, but it took a while. "I was holding my head down weeping. Ten minutes later I felt Brien's arms around me. He said, 'I'm so sorry baby, please forgive me, that will never happen again, I promise.' holding me tight, I calmed down. When I looked into his suffering face I believed him, and he drove me home."

They sat on the chair listening to the boats coming in and out of the Sausalito harbor offering calm. "A few days later Brien told me that after Judge Cleaver had died he was convinced he had been murdered. He was supposed to have met him at the Roosevelt golf club for lunch having become friends.

"When he arrived, he saw Cleaver bent over on the club's restaurant table. The medics has just arrived putting him on the floor giving him C.P.R. to no avail. Brien said on impulse, he hurried to the table where a cup of coffee had been spilled and with his handkerchief wiped the coffee up, putting it in a small plastic bag and hurried off.

"He said he took the handkerchief to the lab for Glover the technician to examine. From his examination he said that the coffee possessed a fast-acting poison enough to kill a horse.

"Brien said that he reported what he had done to his boss and gave him the name of lab examiner with its results. Just as he was leaving the office he had glanced back and saw his boss toss everything in the trash.

"He wrote his letter of resignation, then retrieved what had been tossed in the trash and made the decision to hand it over to the police for investigation. Brien said he left London hours later and spent a month vising a friend in Costa Rica. Thereafter he practiced law in Michigan before working in Los Angeles as their lead prosecutor before being recruited here."

"Did he ever follow up on that situation?" asked Autumn.

"He never told me, and I sure as hell never asked. Brien's a brilliant procurator and has never lost a case."

They continued their walk in silence returning to Autumn's home. "How about breakfast?"

"Some other time. I really feel so much better speaking to you about this. I don't want anything I've told you to put a damper on your experience with Brien. He's a wonderful guy. I love being his law assistant." Autumn was grateful that Claire had confided in her and continued to process what she had been told. No matter, she wanted to get to know Brien.

Alonzo ran up the backstairs to Barbieri's office.

"Come in," he said.

Barbieri despised Alonzo intensely more than anyone in his life. Alonzo's father Mancini was his boss and he had always wanted to kill both of them the worst way.

"Did the job on the Manchester boys," Alonzo announced proudly.

"You fucking did what?"

"That's what my dad wanted me to do, teach them all a lesson. Murdered the Wongs, too. They won't be a problem for my dad in court."

Barbieri reached for his gun as Alonzo raced down the stairs into his new Chevy headed to Alpine, Texas, where he had family and to be safe. Barbieri sank in his chair holding his head in his hands, trying to get a hold of himself. Judge Manchester's twin boys went to St. Vincent's private school. Chief Begay's kids went there, and his kid went there. He lit up a cigar smoking like a chimney, tossing the butt in the waste basket. It immediately caught on fire, putting it out with his leftover coffee. Shit was going to hit the fan. If Chief Begay found out who killed Judge Manchester's twin boys, Begay would go after Alonzo and strangle him with his bare hands, cop or no cop. Barbieri would have killed Alonzo long ago except he was Mancini's crazy son. He hated Mancini. He had murdered a retired bishop for raising hell about his new casino and got away with the hit. The bishop was only doing his job. No one gave a fuck if the casino was a cesspool. Barbieri needed Mancini killed and he'd have Duke, a lifer in jail, do the job with no time to waste.

Alonzo was exhausted from driving three days to his grandmother's house in Alpine, Texas. He had to get out of the United States and go where the mob wasn't. He had a valid passport. He had lots of cash. He liked Canada, but it was too close. He thought about Colombia. Perfect only for now.

Barbieri knew Alonzo was headed to Texas. He called Lewis, his contract killer there, and hired him to find Alonzo and kill him. Barbieri waited anxiously for news that evening.

Finally, the phone rang.

"Bad news," Lewis said. "Alonzo took off last night. No doubt out of the country. He was staying with his elderly grandmother. I spoke to her in Italian. She told me she didn't know where he went. When she left the house, I searched her place from top to bottom, found a note on her kitchen table. Alonzo wrote that he was visiting someone out of town, thanking her."

Barbieri was shocked. "Where do you think he went?"

"If I were him, I'd get the fuck out of the states and go to another country definitely not Italy."

"Where do you want your money sent?"

"The usual."

"Done."

Killing Alonzo had become zilch. Barbieri felt angry and depressed sucking the marrow out of his bones. He thought about Bella, his twenty-five-year-old beautiful, young wife, and their two-year-old child. He thought of Bella's eight-year-old niece put in her care since the death of her sister. Now he was stuck in San Francisco, and it was impossible to leave. He wanted out of the mafia and so he could do whatever the hell he wanted. *Impossible.* Once in the mob, you became a lifer until death. When the old police chief retired, Begay arrived with a blowtorch burning the decay in the police department to ashes and going after the likes of him.

He'd have to attend the burial services with Bella for Judge Manchester's twins. Bella had no idea he was mafia. He adored her. With the murder of Judge Manchester's twin boys, Begay would be on his scent like ravenous snakes. He thought about his former innocent life, graduating from UCLA with a degree in economics. But then he became greedy, wanting fast money, no thanks to Molo, a mafia friend. Molo drove a Maserati, with girls at his beck and call. He was very wealthy and Barbieri dreamed of being like him. Within a short period of time, he was immersed in the mafia.

Barbieri paced back and forth thinking about the love of his life, and his innocent wife Bella. He had never loved any woman as much. It didn't matter that he was twenty years older. He opened the window. He needed more than fresh air.

Bella was a devout Catholic and would be shocked if she knew about his mobster life. She loved her volunteer work at St. Vincent's school. People with money and influence enrolled their children there regardless if they were Jews, Muslims, or criminals, wanting a high level of education for their kids. It was an elite school, known for winning state championships in music, science, and sports.

The children and parents at St. Vincent's would no doubt be devastated by news of the deaths of the Manchester twins loved by everyone. He felt that if Begay wasn't a cop he'd nail him to a cross. He threw his pack of cigars in the trash. Bella hated his smoking, and he'd have to shower and change his clothes before going home. He needed a plan. Fast. Who the fuck could he trust? No one. He flushed his goldfish down the toilet, and took a shower before going home. He thought about the alternatives, which were all dangerous and impossible. There was a contract killer highly sought after and very vicious. He'd take a change and see if he'd do what he wanted.

Chapter 7

Barbieri hurried to his Aston Martin where a grey car with a tough-looking man standing next to a police car flashed his police badge and gun. Begay had just sent him a message in blood. He knew he'd be watched 24/7. Absolutely. When he arrived home, the cop that had followed him parked in front of his house.

He knew the drill. He'd be watched night and day and then followed in plain sight. In no time, the cops would dress in their police uniforms, which would be easy for Bella to see. He had to think of something to tell his wife. He was in fucking trouble.

Brien rose late the next morning thinking about his evening with Autumn. He was planning on calling her when his phone rang. It was Claire.

"I'm at your front door for Christ's sake. Why haven't you been answering the phone?"

"Be there in a second," he said, rushing to get dressed. When he let Claire into his living room, her eyes were bloodshot. She looked at him. "Jesus, you don't know?"

"Know what?"

"Judge Manchester's nine-year-old twin boys were murdered. They were found in Pillar Cemetery's mausoleum." It took a while before he could speak. Claire wiped her eyes.

"Tell me all you know," Brien said.

Two days later, on Saturday at noon, the funeral services for the twins were held at St. Ann's Cathedral in San Francisco. The church was filled to capacity with plainclothes officers sitting in each pew. Judge Manchester had recently been selected as a Supreme Court Justice but had declined. The word was she didn't want such a high-profile life.

Everyone watched as Judge Manchester entered the church. She looked regal, a tall, light-skinned Black woman. She wore a long, white silk dress with a long, black lace veil. Her elderly parents walked beside her. She was raised in Alabama, graduating with honors with a law degree from Duke University in Durham, NC, where she had been a track and field star, having achieved her education on her own.

Judge Manchester came from humble stock with hard-working parents, both janitors and cleaners, long since retired. They were now provided for by their daughter who bought them their first home. They no longer had any financial concerns, thanks to their only child, who had invested her money wisely and no longer had a need to work for the rest of her life. But Nala decided to become an attorney then a Judge, soon revered for her ability to see both sides, the defensive and prosecutorial.

In the front row sat Judge Nala Manchester with her parents. To the left of them were the governor's representative, John Rogers, and Mayor Reynolds and his wife. Chief Begay and Deputy Chief Rowling, sat behind them. No children were allowed to attend the funeral.

Judge Manchester had presided over many complex national white collar crime cases of embezzlement, securities fraud to mention a few that often involved wealthy members of society. Many in attendance reflected their appreciation of her work.

The cathedral was filled to capacity with eight hundred people. Ten-foot-stained glass windows were on the right and left sides of the cathedral including large statues of Jesus, and the saints. Gold lettered stations of the cross were on the left side of the walls and the smell of Frankincense gently wafted through the cathedral. The large altar was covered with white linen and tall candlesticks.

Cardinal Kyle, bishops and clergy, sat near the altar with St. Vincent's school's nuns and priests. The frustrated media were not allowed in the cathedral, feeling shafted as they stood outside past the long entry stairs.

Begay had acknowledged Howard Daley, head of the Prosecutor's office, and Brien Hogan and his assistant, Claire Hobbins. The archbishop entered the sanctuary and the choir began singing "Amazing Grace." Everyone stood and turned watching the two small mahogany caskets being rolled into the church. Tears flowed. Barbieri and his young wife Bella sat in the rear pew watching Judge Manchester kiss the caskets of her beloved twin boys.

"Life is not fair," began Cardinal Kyle, "and let us be consoled that these precious children are with their Divine Savior." Judge Manchester walked up the altar steps to the podium showing strength and resolve. She pulled back her long black veil, revealing her face drenched with tears. At 5'10", she was a stunning-looking woman with no need for makeup.

Everyone edged forward in their seats to hear her speak. "My beloved nine-year-old twin boys, Booker and Calvin, loved laughing in the rain and running in the sunshine." She paused, gathering her strength. "Who would think that they would be so violently taken from my life and from yours?" Brien full of anger, frustration, and sadness, hadn't attended a Catholic church since college, but his assistant, Claire, was a devout Catholic. Brien tried to pray. He tried to mouth the Ave Maria.

Howard Daley whispered, "We'll get through this together," squeezing his arm.

When the mass and religious services were over the small caskets were moved slowly down the long church aisle.

Judge Manchester stopped and turned to Begay whispering, "Please walk with me." She wanted everyone to know that Chief Begay would bring justice for her beloved children. He walked beside her with the gait of a tough-ass general. The church grew stone quiet with everyone given to rapt attention absorbing her message.

In the back sat Shadow, Begay's half-brother of the Navajo nation, and also a sheriff in Montana who also worked occasionally in Yellowstone National Park. From time to time, he did undercover jobs for his brother when needed.

Autumn sat in the back of the church, watching Chief Begay walk down the aisle with Judge Manchester. She left the church and quickly made her way to her car. On the windshield was an envelope. *"I would like to meet with you tomorrow at Gills restaurant in Sausalito,"* followed by a private phone number. She inhaled deeply. What had she done? It took some time to get a hold of herself.

She would meet with Begay and hope to God for the best. He had said noon. No matter. Gills had terrific food from dawn to dusk.

Barbieri had his eye on that "witch" Autumn as she walked out of the church. He despised her for putting him on trial with Mancini though nothing came out of it. He should have killed the bitch when it was easy. Shadow stood in the back with his full attention on Barbieri, having been briefed by his brother about his suspicious behavior and criminal history.

Judge Manchester and her family rode in a limousine to the cemetery where every inch had previously been searched by police, helicopters, and police dogs. Begay had also brought in the military to protect the cemetery, not wanting to take anything for granted.

Before the funeral procession arrived, a black SUV edged toward the cemetery, but was stopped by a young soldier, who pointed his gun in the driver's face.

"Are you fucking blind? Signs all over are prohibiting entry. Step out of your car," said the soldier. "Take off your sunglasses."

"Who gives you the right to order me around? Just driving around."

The soldier dragged the man in his forties and dressed in a grey suit out of his SUV. Immediately he was surrounded. The truck was checked. In the cab of the truck were towels covering three rifles and two revolvers. The man was cuffed and taken away.

The police helicopter made its final sweep over the cemetery and the surrounding areas. When the limousine entered the cemetery, the soldiers snapped to attention, saluting.

Soon, it was learned that the grey SUV had been stolen from an eighty-year-old man living in Berkeley. The driver had no identification. They took his photo and fingerprints at the station then downloaded them into the U.S. database. When the officers went back to his cell, the mystery man was dead. The medics and forensic team were trying to find out what happened. "Maybe he died from a heart attack," said one of the medics but no one knew for sure.

Chapter 8

Chief Begay had requested Titan, a tenacious five-year-old bloodhound with an unshakeable drive from the LAPD, to be brought in to help sniff cars at the funeral. He had an enviable reputation given his powerful nose. Bella, his Belgian Malinois, that he raised from a pup and known for her speed and fearlessness, was also on the scene patrolling the parking lots with Officer Noah, and alongside of the cathedral. In a short time Titan identified a man running from his car outside of the parking lot with a rifle.

The man took off with Titan in hot pursuit. It was then that Officer Noah released Bella to race into the bushes finding the man hiding behind a large rock barking and biting him on his legs and neck until a blast of gunshots sounded. The officer found Bella lying on top of her assailant with Titan the bloodhound licking her. Whimpering. The man had turned his gun on himself. Officer Noah held her in his arms next to his heart stricken with grief.

Begay and Shadow were walking to Begay's truck when Officer Noah Bella's handler ran to him.

"I'm so sorry," he said handing Begay his dog's badge and collar. "She took the fuck down. Her body's been taken to the Troy Veterinarian Hospital."

Begay ran to his truck, tears running down his face. In the distance Barbieri watched, smiling.

Troy Veterinarian Hospital was closed for the afternoon except for emergencies. Dr. Melvin motioned for Begay and Shadow to go to Room D where deceased animals were taken. They both entered the room. The lights were dimmed, but Begay recognized his beloved Bella. Begay wept, caressing and kissing Bella. Shadow chanted Native American songs for the departed animal. "We see you run with the great bison, we see you play with our children, but no more until we meet in the land of beauty," brushing his eagle feathers over her body. Begay covered his dog with his leather Army jacket and gave instructions to Dr. Melvin regarding preparations for Bella's police funeral at his ranch.

The assailant's body was driven to the morgue, and his car searched, devoid of any identification or information, except for takeout from McDonalds. But his prints were everywhere and the forensic team began their work. It didn't take long to find out that the car and its driver Nick Costello were from Albany, New York. He was a mob boss with a horrific rap sheet, having done only one year in Rikers Island after getting out of a twenty-year sentence due to a technicality. They had no evidence why he was at the funeral but Begay felt he was there to kill someone and maybe Judge Manchester.

Mayor John Reynolds recalled having interviewed many candidates, all highly qualified and eager to become San Francisco's new chief of police. But there was only one that he was seriously interested in. The mayor just needed to convince Begay who hadn't applied was the right man to become the new Chief of the San Francisco Police Department.

He had flown to Texas to meet Begay. Before meeting him, Mayor Reynolds was blown away by his background, education, and achievements. It took a miracle to persuade Begay to consider coming to San Francisco to meet with him on a Sunday morning. He remembered taking Begay on a tour of the various police stations, wanting him to know what he was getting himself in to. They walked into the smoke-filled rooms, reeking of disorder and deterioration. If the mayor knew anything about Begay, he knew that he thrived on challenges, and this was one for the books.

Back at his office Mayor Reynolds had watched Begay smiling, maybe a good sign maybe a bad one. Begay had already done his research about the previous Chief and his officers and their history, including the Mayors. The mayor remembered their conversation like it had taken place yesterday. "If I so choose to be your next police chief, this is what I demand," commanded Begay. *Christ, Begay had said "demand," not what he wanted or intended to do.* At that moment the mayor's chest muscles tightened. Begay wanted close to one million dollars, give or take, to do what needed to be done. In less than one year Mayor Reynolds would be running for Governor and he needed to get the police departments in line. Begay had waited a while before giving him his answer. Finally, he said yes. "I'll take the job. In a few months, you won't recognize this police department." The mayor had a special fund for such a situation.

Within two weeks, Begay moved his family, wife and two children, three horses, ten goats, and two dogs to a ranch outside of the city, paid in total from his special fund. On occasion Begay invited Mayor Reynolds to his ranch, but the mayor prudently refused to ride Begay's Arabians. The mayor was proud of his decision to hire Begay comforted that he continued to refuse job offers from around the county.

But now, Mayor Reynolds had to deal with the heartbreaking murder case of Judge Manchester's twin boys and also the Wongs. He wasn't a religious man, but since all this shit happened, he started attending mass every Sunday and even began saying his rosary now a devote Catholic.

The morning after the funeral, Begay sat grimly in his chair, rocking back and forth, trying to put the death of his dog to rest.

"Let's think about who would benefit from these recent deaths," Begay said to his Assistant Chief Rowling. "It has to be mob boss Mancini getting Alonzo, his nutcase son, to do the murders. I don't think Barbieri had anything to do with them, but sure as hell, he'll go after Alonzo and get him killed one way or another. We have to find Alonzo before Barbieri does and murders him."

"Any ideas who can help us out?" asked Rowling.

"I have a friend in Scotland Yard. He might be able to help."

"Good. Let's hope for the best, and as my mom used to say hope don't dance with the dead," said Rowling.

Chapter 9

O fficer Carey drove two blocks from the Wongs house and parked down the block, ecstatic that Begay had entrusted him with investigating the Wong and Manchester murders. The only good thing about this case was that Spenser had been assigned as his assistant. Spenser's family owned Russo Restaurant, and Carey needed to gain weight. He also loved Italian food.

Carey sat in the car and took off his cap, feeling the thick undergrowth of hair on the back of his neck. He was tired of shaving it all off and decided to let his hair grow out.

He was acutely aware that some of the officers made fun of him, calling him "twitchy" and "scarecrow" behind his back, but Chief Begay treated him with respect and so did Rowling. Yet Carey had also been doing all he could in his power to stop stuttering, and jumping at the sound of a sudden noise. He had also recently gained ten pounds though he wanted to gain another fifteen. And, unbeknownst to Chief Begay, Carey had been learning Spanish from his landlord and their housekeeper, planning on surprising the chief by speaking to him in his native language. He was determined to pull his life together. Damn, he just turned twenty-five.

From the moment of his birth, Carey's life had been challenging. As an infant, Carey had been abandoned on the doorstep of an orphanage. It was a difficult environment to grow up in, and some of the kids could be cruel. In exchange for protection from big bad Rosco, Carey had helped the older boy with his studies and he was not a successful sportscaster. Carey was determined to find the murder killers and prove himself to be a mature, confident police detective. He knew Begay trusted him with this case because he had been very successful with every assignment given and determined to solve these murders. He flashed his badge at the officers sitting in their patrol car on the other side of the street and walked up the steps to the Wongs house. Before entering, he spotted a young boy hiding in a bush on the side of the house.

"How's it going?" Carey asked, waving at the kid.

"Ok."

"What's your name?"

"Salvador."

"I was wondering if you saw anyone around here some nights ago?" For a beat the kid hesitated.

"Easy does it. I'm a police officer, and I'm trying to find out who killed Mr. and Mrs. Wong."

"I won't get in trouble, will I?"

"No, but you'll be really super helpful." Salvador moved slowly toward Carey, out of sight from the patrol car.

"I wasn't supposed to be out that night," Salvador confessed. "I went to a dance and biked back home, staying back a ways so no one could see me. Then this man, tall and skinny, runs up the stairs. Never seen him before. He stops, looks around, and fucking pees in that planter where you're standing, pulls down his pants and plays with his dick letting loose. I was crazy shocked. Couldn't move."

"You say that planter with a small bush in it?"

"Yeah."

"Anything else?"

"Then he went to the front door, using something to get it. I left real quiet. Saw his gun sticking out of his jacket pocket."

"Did you tell anyone what you saw?"

"Hell no. Just you now. Will I get in trouble?"

"No. I'm going to toss you my card. If you need anything call me," Carey said, watching Salvador run inside his house.

It took a while for Carey to regain his composure. He took out his flashlight, put on his gloves, and started looking in the potted plant, finding a large tissue, then putting it in a plastic bag, before going into the house. According to the forensic team, the killer wore gloves. When Carey went inside of the house, he found out that the new forensic team didn't go through the house, just the bedroom where the bodies had been. He couldn't believe that was the only place they had searched. In their report they stated they had checked through the whole house. He opened the refrigerator. It was a mess, bottles open and food all over. Carey knew what he'd discovered in the potted plant and the tissue could be the break they were looking for, but he was seriously upset that the forensic team did not search the refrigerator, or the kitchen trash, nor the rest of the house.

Chapter 10

Carey waited with Begay for the two new forensic investigators, Rocco and Ace, to arrive.

"You did a lousy job at the Wongs house," said Carey.

They laughed. Begay allowed Carey to confront them.

"Says who?"

"I do. I'm the lead detective in the Wongs murder case. Read your report. Why didn't you go through the house, the refrigerator and trash? What's worse you lied that you had in your report."

They didn't answer.

"Only the Wongs bedroom was important," Rocco said.

"In your report you claimed to have checked the entire house," retorted Carey.

They grew quiet.

"An eyewitness informed me that he saw a man peeing and masturbating on the potted plant by the front door."

They bent over laughing. "You have a nutcase eyewitness no doubt."

"My witness is more credible then you two are. You didn't do your job," continued Carey, with all the authority he could muster. For the first time in his life, he felt in touch with his anger.

Rocco lost it and went after Carey when Begay's back was turned. Big mistake. He landed on the floor with Begay's boot kicking his ribs. Then Ace hit Carey hard on his nose, causing blood to gush down his neck. Begay yelled, "Kick him in the shins," and Carey did. Ace dropped to the floor. Both men were read their rights then arrested for assaulting officers. And fired.

An ambulance was called to take care of Carey.

"Nose not broken or ribs," the medics said. "He's in shock and needs lots of rest."

"I'll have Spenser take you home to recuperate," Begay said, trying to console Carey. "Don't come back until you are really, and I mean *really* feeling better. Then I'll have someone at the gym teach you how to street fight and learn how to defend your-self without the use of a gun, real different from what's taught in the academy. Believe me it prevents cops from killing kids with their guns."

Carey whispered, "I'd like that lots, Chief."

After Carey was taken home by Spenser, Begay called Miguel, a tough kid raised in East LA, telling him about Carey. "He's never been in a fight in his life."

"No problem," Miguel said.

"I don't want him being hurt, or you'll be fucking hurting." Miguel had dealt with Begay before, and it wasn't always pleasant.

"I definitely understand," and he sure as shit meant it.

Next day Carey was at the gym with a swollen face, nose bandaged, and holding up brave. He looked forward to learning how to street fight. Miguel looked him over. "Christ, I can't even find a muscle. I'm putting you on a weightlifting program. You gotta gain at least 20 pounds. No offense, but you look like a sack of bones ready for Halloween."

"I've been working on my weight," Carey said trying to smile. "Good. We'll take it real easy." Begay's threat was still hot in Miguel's brain.

Several days later, Begay was sitting in the back of the gym wiping his face with his towel when Carey came in the gym with Miguel, dressed in protective gear from head to toe. He put his towel to his mouth, laughing uncontrollably.

Later that day Begay met with Rowling.

"No doubt Barbieri knows where Alonzo is or will be very soon. He won't talk to us. That's for damn sure. I feel in my gut he'll try to get him killed. We must act fast. I know someone in Scotland Yard who might help us. Right now, we need more help."

It took a while for Begay to make the call.

"Well, well, old friend. Haven't heard from you in so long. I can hardly recall our bar hopping," Samson laughed.

"I'm trying not to recall," said Begay.

"I understand your top dog at the Yard."

"Yeah, they were kind of desperate," Samson laughed again. He was a brilliant criminologist.

"How's chiefhood treating you these days? Chief here and chief there."

"So, we both follow each other's careers," said Samson.

"Only when I've had a loose end," said Begay. It felt good to laugh with his childhood friend. Samson's family had moved back to England when Samson was seventeen. He graduated from Oxford with a Ph.D. in Criminology. "I need a favor," said Begay.

"Let's see what I can do."

"Judge Manchester's twin nine-year-old boys and the prosecutor's primary witnesses have been murdered. Our forensic match prints found in Barbieri's office that leads to Alonzo, the son of

Mancini, who was tied to these murders and recently killed in jail. I feel his jail murder is tied to mobster Barbieri. No proof.

"Presently Alonzo might still be in the U.S. but most likely left the country, but not to Italy. I'm sending you his rap sheet and photo."

"I'll see where he is hiding no doubt in garbage cans so to speak. You know it'll cost lots and lots of pesos."

"No problem, thanks to our mayor who has deep pockets."

"Good. I'm right on it," said Samson. "We'll nail Alonzo before he's on the hunt for more victims. If anyone can help us it's Samson," he said to Rowling.

"Good move," said Rowling.

Later that day Carey fully recovered spoke to Begay in the hallway. "Just want to thank you for setting me up with Miguel and for my new office."

"You deserve it."

Carey's office had two large pine tables, file cabinets, computers, phones, and even a cot with a small window. The mayor had given Begay over a million dollars for the police building's extensive renovation. He wanted his officers to work hard, play hard, and be in superior shape thanks to their new gym on the third floor complete with personal trainers. And this included an extensive police education fund.

No one called Carey a kid anymore, having filled out, growing a good head of hair, and speaking with authority and often in Spanish. He had been physically transformed from working out in the gym. He even had a girlfriend. One day at lunch Carey took out his wallet showing everyone Maureen, a 5'8" brunette with wavy hair past her shoulders, hazel eyes, and a charming smile. *Shock* was a small word given their reactions.

Chapter 11

B rien was eager to talk to Autumn on the phone.

"Can't believe it," she said. "Just thinking about you."

"That makes two of us. So, how about dinner at my place? Leonardo is a fine cook and you'll have a wonderful time. I can pick you up and return you home?" He waited anxiously for her answer.

"I would love that."

"How's 6?"

"Perfect."

Brien couldn't believe he was feeling a bit nervous.

Leonardo calmed him down. "Relax. She'll love the risotto and wine."

For Brien, the hours dragged until dinner. Finally, he drove to Autumn's cottage, anticipating that Winston would give him more than the evil eye. Autumn opened the door.

"Where's dear Winston?"

"At my friend's house. He's in love with Bonnie's poodle." Brien drove her to his home. "I smell something delicious," she said entering his house.

"Leonardo has prepared risotto, hope you like it."

He led her to the dining room where white candles glowed on the white linen table. "I've never in my life tasted such delicious food," she said sipping her wine. Later he lead her outside where they sat on cushioned chairs, watching the sun allow the moon to take its place. In a short time a slight breeze began to sweep through the maple tree branches.

"Your home is heavenly," she said.

"It took six months to find it. Gives me so much happiness from being a procurator." Brien's house was a Spanish colonial house with large elm trees in the front offering peacefulness and beauty. The floors were crafted from exotic oak wood and the walls were painted a cream white. There was a large white marble fireplace in the living room and small cozy fireplaces in all the bedrooms. Throughout the home were green, healthy potted plants that offered contentment and with exotic rugs from India.

He had moved his lawn chair closer to hers, holding her hand and began kissing her hungerly. He wanted her in his bed. Instead, he said, "I can take you home now if you wish."

"Take me home," she said. "It's been a wonderful evening. If your amazing cook gets weary of working for you, send him over to me."

"Don't think so," he said, both laughing.

He drove her home and walked her up the path to her house smelling the sweet scent of jasmine.

"Come in with me," she said leading him to her bedroom. He couldn't remember being so consumed with passion, holding her in his arms, kissing her all over.

When he awoke the next morning, the sun had greeted the day with cool air filling her cottage.

"Hungry?" Autumn called out to him. "I sure am."

"Last night was special for me," he said.

"And for me as well," she agreed, handing him a plate filled with pancakes and blueberries.

"I don't want this to be a one-time thing," he said. "I want to be with you regardless of my crazy work life."

Autumn took his hand. "We'll take it easy. I want that as well."

She watched him drive off, hating to see him leave. Winston had come back and growled smelling Brien's scent in her bedroom.

"You'll like him, jealous boy," she said, but Winston didn't wag his tail.

Begay had planned a meeting with Autumn at Gills restaurant at noon, so she had a little time to get ready. When she arrived, she was just in time to see Begay getting out of his truck. He was wearing civilian clothes. When he walked inside of the restaurant, people turned their heads, wondering if he was a movie star.

"I appreciate your coming given such short notice," he said to Autumn when he approached his table.

"No problem at all."

"Let's order lunch."

They ate in silence until Begay spoke. "I know about your remarkable record, once a police detective but unjustly treated. Under my watch, you would have been a high-ranking police officer," Begay said, watching her eyes water. "You did a remarkable job getting that fuck Mancini in jail. Perhaps you know he's been killed?"

"No, I didn't. Too bad. I wanted him to suffer long in prison."

"That makes two of us."

"The investigation into who murdered the Wongs and Judge Manchester's twin boys is urgent and dangerous," Begay told Autumn. "Everything points to Mancini's son Alonzo. I need you to go to Barbieri's office and see if you can find any information on where Alonzo might be hiding. We must act fast because that fuck will be leaving the states fast, if not already." Begay didn't mention his contact with Scotland Yard.

"Carey's in charge of this investigation," Begay continued, "but given your background, you're better for what I need at this point. You'll only report to me without exception. No one will know about our arrangement except my deputy police chief Rowling." Autumn knew he didn't expect her to ponder long if she'd go for it.

"I'll do my best," she said, her knees quivering a bit nervously. "Here's my private number. Your investigation is strictly confidential. If at any time you feel your life is in danger, tell me. I'll take care of the situation before you take your next breath. This is what I want you to do," he continued, handing her a slip of paper with his private number. Then, he pushed a bag that contained her old S&W Magnum 19 onto the table toward her. "Carry your gun at all times, and it'll save your life."

She took her gun rubbing it like a long-lost friend. "Is it loaded?"

"You gotta know it is."

What she didn't know was that Begay's brother Shadow would be her protector, a man never having failed in any such situations. Just being in Begay's presence and listening to him gave her a sense of security, and she vowed not to fail this critical assignment.

Autumn knew this investigation would be dangerous, yet confident she'd be protected. Shadow had been outside the restaurant, watching.

"Even your dog Winston, your two chickens. and your dear old duck will be protected."

She laughed. "How do you know that?"

"I know most things."

"When do I start?"

"In a few hours. Go to Barbieri's office at 1 am and go through his papers. See what you can find out about his contract killers and about Mancini's family and his deranged son, Alonzo. You must not be there more than twenty minutes then get the hell out."

"Twenty minutes?"

"Yes, or sooner. Be sure to take your gun."

When Autumn got back home after lunch with Begay, she felt a long-lost surge of excitement.

At 1 am Autumn entered Barbieri 's office. The door was unlocked. She scanned the place with her flashlight. The place was all torn up. She opened his unlocked safe, quickly putting the papers on his desk, flipping through them quickly, holding her breath. Bingo. She found what she was looking for: a list of names and contacts with phone numbers and addresses. She used his copy machine and returned everything back in the safe just as it was. She looked at her watch. Christ, she had to hurry.

Autumn had scanned his desk and drawers, then looked out his broken window, startled to see Barbieri getting out of his car parked on the street. There was only one staircase. Briefcase in hand, she ran down flattening her body to the side as he hurried up the stairs, smoking and talking to himself. She waited until he shut his door and ran. His police tail was out of his car flashing his badge, having been warned not to leave his post.

She sprinted like a gazelle to get away, breathing hard and swearing. She dropped the briefcase and was picking it up when two tough guys came out of a bar ready to chase her. She reached for her gun and shocked that she had left it at home. Begay had warned her: "Always carry your gun. Shit happens." She kept running but stopped when she heard someone yelling at the men and turned around.

They froze when a tall, well-built, brown-skinned man threatened them with a gun in hand. "Get back in that bar," he yelled, and they ran in like rabbits. She wanted to thank him, but he disappeared. Once she got back home, she wondered who that man was spreading out the papers on her table, looking at the names for Barbieri's hit men. She'd contacted Begay at five, putting her gun under her pillow, swearing to God almighty to keep it with her even in the bathroom.

Chapter 12

After Begay had finished his workout at the gym, Miguel had asked him to observe Carey's progress. He entered the gym without protective gear and stood on the large mat. A young man his size had attempted to throw him down using a fake knife. Carey was faster and had the man down, wrestling the knife from him in twenty-five seconds. Begay stood clapping, utterly astonished. Miguel was ecstatic, having achieving the seemingly impossible and wanting to give Carey an Olympic gold medal.

Back in his office Carey was hard at work, appreciating the new computer, telephone, file cabinets, and a small oak desk, with pictures of his rabbit and elephants, but he had no photos of family having been raised in orphanage.

He rubbed his fingers on his desk recalling the drastic changes that had taken place in the police building after Begay had been appointed their new chief. The large second floor had broken tile on the floors and was devoid of windows for air and light. All the working desks swayed back and forth. The walls were painted a dull grey and the ceiling lights blinked off and on.

The building's renovation was radical. During that time the officers worked in the basement, watching carpenters, tile workers, and painters transform the second-floor large room, including five private offices.

An entire wall on the second floor had been removed and re-placed with large windows, offering sunlight warmth, and sweeping views of the park filled with elm and oak trees and play areas for families and children.

The officers had spacious workstations with soundproof panels, preventing them from hearing and seeing each other. Everyone had new pine tables for their computers and telephones. He remembered when Begay had led them up the stairs to see the mind-blowing renovations for the first time.

The officers were utterly speechless. "Your work is difficult and unrelenting," Begay said. "It's my intention to ease as much of your stress as much as possible. I understand and appreciate the challenges of being a police officer and having someone like me to deal with," he added bringing laughter among the officers.

"No smoking inside this building," he continued. "And if you brag too much, we'll need to deal with traffic control, stopping other police departments itching for your jobs." Rare as it was, Begay smiled. His officers clapped. It was a new day thought Carey, who knew he needed to get back to work, but he just couldn't help reliving the memories. In time they learned that Mayor Reynolds had received a generous donation, allowing Begay to achieve the impossible. The next day the officers arrived at work with a skip and their work improved quickly. Even the hard-core smokers soon gave up their habit and the sparse few that remained smoking by the trash cans feeling like outcasts. Of course, they were.

In Begay's office was a stunning picture of his great-grand-mother, a woman of the Comanche tribe, a skilled rider standing strong by her horse, and by a white buffalo. Every time Carey went into his office regardless of his problems, he felt happy.

The governor insisted that Begay and Carey come to Sacramento for a meeting. Furious, Begay rode in the helicopter with Rowling. "I didn't bring Carey with us," he said to Rowling, "because this is a serious waste of his precious time as ours."

"Why does he want us to come to Sacramento anyway?"

"He's a jerk and a control freak. That's why," said Begay.

"I told the governor we can't stay for lunch," continued Begay. "Fact is I dislike him so intensely I'd get serious heartburn. When we needed money, this is what the fuck said. Don't come to me sniffling for money. Find it yourself."

"You gotta calm down," said Rowling worried that Begay would lose it. "Maybe we return back and make up some excuse."

"Too fucking late."

The helicopter began its descent on a cloudy day in Sacramento. They were led into the governor's study, both observing the beautiful mahogany walls and desk.

The governor smiled. "So glad you could come. Where's Carey?"

"A critical situation developed and he's unable to be here," said Begay. "Whatever you want to know I can easily update you."

Governor Nash's face grew red. "I don't give a damn. Carey was supposed to be here and brief me personally." Rowling stood closer to Begay. The governor yelled, "I asked that he come. I am the governor of the state of California." Begay knew Mayor Reynolds had just beat Nash in the election. "I'll have you both removed from your positions immediately."

"No, you won't," said Begay voice raised. They left quickly, listening to Nash yelling profanities.

Begay's mood in the helicopter was bad. "There's no damn reason we had to visit that fuck in the first place."

"I concur," said Rowling." He took out a set of cards. "How about a game of poker? Bet I'll beat you," Rowling said, knowing he'd lose regardless of Begay's mood.

Chapter 13

In the afternoon Begay addressed his officers.

"Give me your attention. Carey my lead detective in the Wong and Manchester twins murder cases will give you his progress report." The officers edged forward in their seats eager to listen to the new Carey, who no longer pulled his hair or stuttered and shifted his feet back and forth.

"These homicide cases are of the utmost importance. Although I am leading this investigation all of us have a serious role in solving these cases as quickly as possible. In thirty minutes, we will podcast these posted phone numbers for citizens to call in their tips and you'll be rotating to respond to these calls," said Carey.

"I want you to study this sketch from an eyewitness who saw this man at the door of the Wongs house. We have every reason to believe that we are looking for Alonzo, the son of Mancini, recently killed in jail.

"We want to find him before he leaves San Francisco and maybe our country. This photo will be given to all networks and police stations as we speak. I am available if any of you have questions. Although we are at the early stages of this investigation, time is of the essence. Let's work as a team to prosecute those responsible for these hideous murders to the full extent of the law." Carey stepped back and the room was silent.

Then, Begay asked, "Any questions?" No hands went up. Everyone was trying to process the new Carey as well as their current responsibilities.

Spenser followed Carey into their office.

"Let's get rid of that cot," Carey said. "Replace it with a card table for our lunch. I need to keep gaining weight. How about getting lasagna with a blueberry shake and a large piece of cake for yourself?"

"I'll get it from my family's restaurant," Spenser said, hurrying out of the office. Having lost twenty pounds, now with Begay's healthy regime, Spenser knew he had to be careful. He knew the cake was just for him, but he'd get a small one. Maybe. He returned with a large bag. The officers could smell the lasagna.

One called out, "Come over here. That's for me." Spenser walked into Carey's office, shutting the door, putting out the sign, "Do Not Disturb," both chowing down in no time.

Early next morning Brien and Claire had parked their cars in the underground garage, preparing for a meeting with their boss Howard Daley. Begay hurried down the stairs to his patrol truck, glancing in their direction and sped off. He thought about his last conversation with Judge Manchester the night before. She had thanked him for walking down the aisle in the funeral procession and for offering her private protection.

Begay had reassured Howard Daley, head of the prosecutor's office, that they would find who murdered the Wongs and the Manchester children. But, for the time being, they didn't know the details of the investigation. Brien and Claire sat in Howard Daley's office. He said, "Since Mancini is dead, everything has changed. We must wait until Begay finds the primary suspect believed to be Alonzo, involving a new case and witnesses. In the meantime, both of you can take some time off."

Carey had shown Begay a telephone lead that Alonzo was in Friona, a small town in Texas. He spoke to Police Chief Jamestown.

"We might be too late. Alonzo has been moving around faster than a lizard," said Begay.

"We're on it. I'll keep you informed," said Jamestown.

Begay and Rowling went to the park hoping fresh air would calm Begay down, not close.

"Every time when I think about that fuck, I want to kill him with my bare hands. Manchester's little boys were so much fun. Everyone loved them at St. Vincent's school. My children adored them."

"I feel we'll catch him somehow," said Rowling.

"Maybe yes, maybe not. Barbieri is being watched 24/7, thought about bringing him in for questioning, but he'd lie down his pants, a waste of time. I've been anxious to hear from Samson, Head of Scotland Yard. If anyone can find Alonzo, he can, and even a bedbug in a pile of shit."

Chapter 14

Begay entered the large office room where twenty-five officers were working at their desks.

"Your attention please," Begay shouted.

The officers were suddenly taken aback when they noticed Begay's military pistol at his side.

"We have a serious situation," he informed the officers, updating them on the most recent happenings regarding the murders. "I want you to wear your guns and take them home under my rigid rules of engagement. This is our situation," said Begay.

Begay told Autumn to meet him outside of her home. He'd be in an unmarked police sedan at 5 that evening. On the dot he arrived. She sat inside his car, holding her briefcase tightly. He drove ten blocks away.

"How did it go down?" he asked. "I reviewed everything in Barbieri's office, got into his open safe. His place was shocking, all torn up, window broken, and when I looked out the window, Barbieri was getting out of his car. I got out real fast."

She didn't tell him about the guys at the bar or the man who had threatened them with his gun. He studied the list of names. "Good job. I'll get right on it." He pulled out a Glock 42, a small pistol which fit easily in a woman's purse. "Carry this in your purse at all times regardless of your other gun." She took it quickly. "Something has just come up. It's delicate and dangerous. I don't want to pressure you into doing it. You can refuse."

"Tell me."

"Know a police officer by the name of Sid?"

She pounded her fist on this dashboard. "When I was fighting off that fuck trying to rape me in the shower, Sid was in the corner laughing." Begay offered her pause.

"I'll tell you what is involved. I understand if you don't want to do it."

"Hell, yes."

"When?"

"Tonight."

Sid was one of several officers taking turns watching Barbieri's house. Autumn parked across the street. Watching. Within the hour he went to the front door, quickly handed Barbieri a folder. Both men slapped each other on the shoulder with Sid receiving a thick envelope, no doubt cash.

"Damn," she whispered. An extremely drunk young girl came out of a house, weaving across the street by Sid's car. He got out and grabbed her, pulling up her dress, his dick out pushing to get inside her.

"No. No." she cried.

Autumn raced out of her car knocking Sid to the ground, hammering him on the head with her gun and hurried the girl across the street getting her back inside the house.

"Don't leave. That man is dangerous," Autumn said. In the worse way Autumn wanted to shoot him. She watched him struggling to get back into his car. Not long afterwards, his replacement came to relieve him. He drove off very slowly, rubbing his head.

Begay had instructed Autumn to phone immediately regardless of the hour. It was now 3 am.

"What's going on?" he asked, briefing him in on what had gone down.

"Good work" he said.

Barbieri had seen Sid attempt to rape the young girl when a woman rushed out of her car to her defense. He noticed the way the woman moved, holding her gun, knocking Sid to his knees. No doubt about it. She was an undercover, tough-ass cop. Shit, they were onto him. He had to get to Albany. He was still in trouble even if Mancini was dead.

Autumn returned home an emotional wreck, sitting in her rocking chair on her porch with Winston trying to comfort her. She wanted to kill that bastard. Shadow watched her from his post wondering how long Autumn would be able to work for Begay. She phoned Brien. Soon after he arrived and tucked her in bed, and thigh to his side sleeping until dawn.

When Sid returned to his apartment, Begay was there. "So, you're the fucking mole," he snarled, taking Sid's badge and gun. He had searched his place from top to bottom. "How long have you been working for Barbieri?" Sid didn't answer. Begay punched him hard in his stomach. It didn't take long for Sid to tell him. "Put your hands behind your back."

"No." Begay punched him again much harder.

"Put your hands behind your back." Sid did and quickly.

Begay thought about the note under his office door, telling him that Sid had gone into Carey's office taking out files and making copies. The next morning Sid's desk had been cleaned out as well as his locker, giving Carey deep satisfaction. Sid was put in jail awaiting trail and no one gave a damn. Officer Carey drove past Sid's apartment where a large Apartment for Rent sign was hanging. Laughing.

Chapter 15

Samson from Scotland Yard updated Begay. "We found Alonzo in Colombia," he reported.

"Colombia?"

"Yes, his mother, long deceased, is from there, and he speaks fluent Spanish. No doubt he's feeling comfy among their criminals."

"This situation has become very dangerous," said Samson. "It's your call if you want to haul him in."

"We have Dragon watching him. He's done successful work for us in the past." Begay knew that capturing Alonzo would involve killings. Was it really worth it?

"Alonzo is being watched, but from my experience we have to act fast. It doesn't matter if Dragon is well paid, he'll sure as shit go for the highest bidder if someone else wants him."

"Will get back to you first thing early tomorrow," said Begay.

"By the way, when do you plan to return my Superman comics?"

"Oh, Christ, resting in my garage. Will be in the mail today." They both started laughing.

Begay had also just learned that Barbieri was at the airport heading to Albany and immediately got a hold of Autumn, knowing she had lived there.

"Did you work in Albany?" he asked her on the phone.

"I was a legal secretary there before going to Fordham University Law School. I only practiced law there for two years."

"Why?"

"Didn't like it."

"Do you have any connections in those parts?" Begay probed. She tried to collect herself.

"I was dating Albert Constantino a police officer at the time. He wanted to marry me, but I wasn't ready haven't spoken to him since."

"Do you think he'd be willing to help us?"

"Maybe."

"We have five hours before Barbieri arrives in Albany."

Begay met Autumn at St. Rita's Catholic Church in the last row of pews. She was nervous shifting back and forth in the pew.

"Give me a moment," Begay said before going outside to talk to Rowling, who told him that Albert Constantino had recently been promoted to Assistant Police Chief in the Albany Police Department. He was 37 years old, graduated from NYU with honors.

"Anything else?" Begay asked.

"Unmarried."

Returning to Autumn, Begay said, "Do you happen to have his phone number? Maybe he can help us."

Autumn shuffled in her purse and found her phone. She dialed his number.

"Well . . . well, it's been a while," Constantino said.

"Yes, it has. Look, this isn't a social call. I'm doing some work for Chief Begay, and he'd like to speak to you."

"Before he does, how have you been these fine days?"

"Wonderful. Love San Francisco."

"A new boyfriend, perhaps?" Begay could see Autumn's face redden.

"As a matter of fact, yes."

"Good for you," he said cheerfully.

Begay took note of her clenched fist.

He briefed Constantino on the developments of the murder cases and the mob boss, Barbieri.

"Damn. What a terrible situation. What can I do for you?"

"Barbieri should be arriving by private jet in five hours give or take. I would like him followed. Once we know what's he's up to, we can formulate a plan."

"Luckily, I'm taking a few days off. Given what you've told me, I'll see what I can do. Let's exchange phone numbers. I assume I just report to you?"

"That's right."

Constantino drove to the airport in nondescript clothing, excited to get away from his position as Assistant Chief of Police, yet aware he had to be very careful. It had been a while since he had experienced such a rush, speeding in his 1976 Mustang to the airport. It was nice hearing from Autumn except for finding out she now has a boyfriend.

It wasn't hard for Constantino to spot Barbieri. He got off of the plane and took off in a black sedan down Madison Ave. heading straight for the city of Rensselaer.

"I don't believe this shit," Constantino said to himself, having followed him to a warehouse devoid of cars except for a black truck. He'd wait for as long as it took having parked out of sight with his gun in his lap. He knew that contract killer Pierre used this warehouse for his meetings. They had tried for years to jail him without success given his high-paid elite attorneys.

Begay and Rowling came up the backstairs and quickly stopped. Why was the room usually so busy with officers now so quiet? Captain George Whitecuff quickly approached Begay.

"The governor is in your office."

"You can't be serious?"

"I sure am. He marched in there like he owns the place." Everyone watched with the office growing quiet. Begay and Rowling rushed into the office, leaving the door wide open.

"Shut your door," snapped the governor.

"No one comes in here without an appointment," said Begay.

"I am the governor. I don't need appointments."

They remained standing.

"Nice renovations you made but that silly Injun on the wall needs to go," said the governor.

Rowling moved closer to Begay, hoping to God he'd keep it together. "She is my beautiful grandmother of the Comanche tribe that I deeply revere, and I'm honored to have her picture hanging on my wall. It's time for you to leave, Mr. Nash."

"Hell, no. I have business to discuss."

"We have been notified that you're no longer the governor of the state of California. Keep the little dignity you have left and get out of my office." Rowling opened the window. The heat in the office had become unbearable. Nash left, mouthing incoherent speech. Rowling followed him out the building and locked the front entry door. He watched Nash approach a car with a chauffeur waiting, but then hurried back, pounding on the front door. Rowling pulled out his gun and pointed it at him. That did it. Nash took off.

Begay drove to his ranch home needing to get a grip on his emotions. He rode his Arabian horse Rara Avis, a stunning beauty with an ebony body, a silver mane into the forest. He slid off his horse and rested his back against the trunk of an old elm tree. He took comfort knowing that he had made progress as the police reformer, and convinced he'd put Alonzo in prison. The sun began to set, offering a blanket of darkness and shades of peace.

Chapter 16

Brien and Claire followed Howard Daley into the back room to meet their new witness, Janet Homes, ringing her hands while sitting on the edge of the cushioned chair.

"Please meet Brien Hogan and Claire Hobbins. They will be asking you a few questions."

"More questions," Janet complained. "Did all of that this morning with some police officer who drove me here. I want all of this done. You're putting my life in danger."

"We're going to take good care of you. You have nothing to fear," said Brien, trying to reassure her.

"You don't understand. Barbieri will kill me when he finds out I'm a witness in the Mancini murder case involving him."

Janet wiped her eyes. Claire sat beside her offering her some Kleenex.

"You'll receive twenty-four-hour protection. You need not worry. Your meals will be served in your guarded room, and, if you want to go anywhere, you will have protection," said Brien.

"How long have you worked for Barbieri?" Claire asked.

"Ten years. As a part-time secretary. During that time my husband died, Barbieri paid for his funeral. He always paid me well in cash. On Fridays, I'd deliver packages to Mancini. But all that changed when I was going up the backstairs to his office to deliver the usual Friday money bag one night. He was yelling at that dear old, retired bishop, admonishing him about the sins of his casino.

"I saw him shoot him in the head."

Janet took a long, slow drink. "I crept down the backstairs and drove back to Barbieri's place returning his money bag, telling him that I had a flat tire. After a couple of weeks, I told Barbieri I wanted to retire and be with my family since my husband had died. He was fine about it giving me ten thousand dollars, wishing me well. I don't want to betray my good friend," she sniffled.

"We understand," Claire said, trying to console the woman.

"No, you don't understand," Janet screamed. "I need to use the restroom."

Claire left the room to take Janet to the restroom. "Looks like we've lost her," said Brien.

When Janet returned, she kept on screaming. "I'm not going to be your fucking witness. Find someone who doesn't give a damn."

"You're free to go," said Brien, being careful not to mention she could be called back as a hostile witness.

"Thank you for your help," said Claire.

"Up yours," Janet said, marching out of the office kicking the door twice.

Later that day, Brien phoned Autumn.

"Let's get together. Tell me when and where."

"You're timing is perfect. How about lunch at Bristol's? I have business thereabouts."

"See you soon." Brien felt happy the stress with Janet gone.

Constantino had followed Barbieri into the seedy part of the city of Rensselaer, watching him hurry into a run-down warehouse. He knew Pierre a notorious contract killer did crime business there. They had tried to nail him for five murders without success, no thanks to his squadron of elite attorneys well paid. He watched him carrying a briefcase and looking around nervously.

A voice in the dark asked Barbieri, "What do you want?"

"I want you to find Alonzo in Colombia and deliver him to me."

"Why?"

Barbieri didn't answer.

"Why?"

"I want to kill him. I want Chief Begay killed too."

The lights flicked on.

Barbieri watched Pierre's eyes turn to flames.

"Are you going to kill me?" Barbieri asked.

"Thinking about it. This is what you're going to do. Go back to San Francisco. I'll decide if and when I'll have you killed. Get the fuck out of here," Pierre yelled, shooting his Remington M14 over Barbieri's head, expecting to get killed but wasn't, maybe tomorrow. He sped off to the airport confused by Pierre's reaction. There was no way he could find another contract killer given their shared network.

Pierre pounded his fists on a rickety card table, despising Barbieri for wanting Chief Begay killed. He remembered when he had joined the Army and met Begay. Both were tough smart-ass kids at eighteen. It felt like yesterday when they were in boot camp with their sadistic officer berating a whimpering skinny, short soldier, beating him furiously with his baton.

Begay ran to the wounded soldier, grabbing the baton out the officer's hand throwing it on the ground, hollering, "You better follow the Army rules and never do what you've just done." In the distance, the commanding officer, who had been watching, ran toward them.

The sadistic officer picked up his baton and went after Begay, who yelled, "Come on asshole. Take me on." The officer tried but failed. Furious, Begay threw him on the ground. The commanding officer approached and addressed the officer in front of the cadets, "See me in my office."

"What's your name?" the commanding officer asked cadet.

"Finn Begay."

"Well, Finn Begay, given the circumstances, you did the right thing."

That day Begay was sent to the Green Berets Special Forces, eventually becoming their elite sniper, making history at age 18. Since then, Pierre had followed Begay's career, knowing he had become an outstanding Chief of Police, while he had become a highly-sought contract killer.

Pierre hadn't wept since he was seven years old. But today it took him a while to get a hold of himself. He called a contact in Colombia, asking him to bring Alonzo to him unharmed. Given the generous pay it sure didn't take long.

Two days later, Pierre drove to the police station in his white Lamborghini with Alonzo, wearing a black cover over his head with zip-tied wrists and ankles. Pierre, wearing a mask, pushed Alonzo out of the car, having previously alerted Begay of his arrival time.

"Who are you?" asked Begay.

Pierre didn't answer. He just got back into his sports car.

"Wait, please. I want to thank you for bringing that fuck in. I wish you a good life with lots of love and laughter," Begay said, putting both hands to his heart the way they always did as kids. Overcome with emotion, Pierre got out of the car, took off his mask, and hugged him.

"I'll always love you, brother," said Begay.

"And so, will I" Pierre answered.

Begay watched his old once-upon-a-time friend drive off. And Pierre felt deep joy for the first time in decades as he stepped into a new life of redemption.

Chapter 17

B rien walked into Bristol's restaurant, finding Autumn sitting in the back by the window.

"How's your real estate business coming along?"

"Getting busier," she said, but that wasn't true since working for Begay. "And you?"

"Better news with the Wong and Manchester murder cases."

Their waiter came to the table and they both ordered chicken sandwiches.

"You said better news?" Autumn asked, hiding the fact that Begay kept her posted. "How good?"

Brien laughed, remembering Autumn had been the police officer responsible for putting Mancini in jail.

"We've learned that Alonzo, Mancini's kid, is the killer of the Manchester's boys and the Wongs, and that Barbieri was responsible for the hit on Mancini in jail. Begay told me that one of Mancini's cellmates confessed to the murder. Alonzo is in jail waiting to be tried."

"Good news at last," she said.

"Would you be up to taking a walk down the street to that small kids park?"

Autumn laughed. "Of course."

He took her hand, which felt warm and comforting. The playground was peaceful as they approached. "Look down the road. There's a roller skating rink," he said. "Can you skate?"

"Sure can," she said.

Autumn made a quick turn on her skates and almost fell over. Brien caught her in his arms and began kissing her passionately for a few seconds.

"Let's get going. Where's your car?" he asked her.

"My neighbor dropped me off," she said.

"I'll drive you home," he offered, putting on music. Both were lost with thoughts of love and passion.

"Allow me to walk you to your door if you can promise that Winston won't attack me."

"Won't," Autumn smiled. "I'm helping him get used to you. Come on in. Here, give him a piece of chicken." Brien dropped the chicken at Winston's paws. The dog lapped it up quickly then went into the yard. Brien quickly folded Autumn into his arms, with passion consuming him. He dared not think beyond the moment.

When Brien awoke, Autumn was sleeping soundly. Brien's arm dangled off of the bed, and he felt Winston's warm tongue licking his hand. At last, we're friends.

Though Brien had had many temporary lovers, Autumn was the only woman he truly loved. He couldn't imagine being with anyone else in his life. But he was afraid to ask her how she felt about him. When the time was right, he knew he would.

He left Autumn's home, and later in the day decided to visit Pillar Cemetery. When he drove through the entrance, he parked his car to the side, then walked up the weedy path. He paused in front of what was once a beautiful mausoleum. It had now sadly been desecrated by the murders of Judge Manchester's children and the Wongs. Brien kicked the stones aside with his boots. In the distance he could hear an owl screeching at him from a tall, oak tree. On the far end of the small graveyard, a tall redwood tree remained strong and resilient despite the graveyard's neglect. From his childhood he loved the way his mother took him to cemeteries while eating candy and listening to her speak of the dead as if she knew each one, and how important it was to revere their lives.

At the end of the graveyard was a grey marble bench large enough for two. Etched onto the bench were the words, "Waiting for You." He couldn't stop laughing, liftings his spirits enormously. He decided to visit one gravesite after the next. He strangely enjoyed visiting this lonely graveyard yearning to be loved as it once was in its glorious and beautiful days. He walked once more through the cemetery, making an unexpected, yet important decision. He was going to buy Pillar Cemetery and restore to its former glory. Although it had grown late in the day, Brien paid a visit to the owner.

"For God's sake," the owner said. "Forgot I even owned it." Within the hour, the man was paid and Brien became its new owner.

The very next morning, Brien hired a young contractor named Hudson to develop a plan for the cemetery's restoration.

"It's going to be very costly given all you want, and damn it's in a hell of a mess."

"Just get it done to my satisfaction with no time to spare."

"Will start within the hour. As you're aware, this will be a tough-ass job given its enormous cleanup, and not to mention everything you want done," said Hudson.

"I am very aware," he said smiling.

Becoming Pillar Cemetery's new owner felt like fatherhood. During most evenings Brien would take his sleeping bag and lay by the tree where the owl perched becoming friends so he could converse with her. "I'm in love," Brien confessed. "Fact is I want to marry Autumn." The owl was silent and seemed to listen. "I fear she doesn't love me. I fear she won't marry me," Brien continued, close to tears. The great old owl began to hoot, calming Brien and helping him enter the deepest realm of peace and sleep.

One morning, at 7 am, Brien awoke to the sound of workmen installing a tall, ornate black iron fence pleasant to the eye, and protect the graveyard along with a stunning ornate iron entry gate. All of the tombstones were being cleaned and polished to a fine glow. Along the fences tall bushes were being planted and new comfortable maple benches installed throughout the cemetery.

Brien hurried out of his sleeping bag and stood before the mausoleum, which would soon be refinished with white alabaster marble. Fresh-smelling green grass and newly hewn pathways would encourage visitors to wander, pause, and admire this place, a gentle reminder that life must not be taken for granted. After the renovations were completed, Brien asked Father Langston from St. John's church to bless the cemetery given that murder victims were found on the site.

"May the Lord bless this restored graveyard and bless its beauty with light, and love, offering peace and comfort to all who come here," prayed the priest.

Begay had entered the cemetery with his brother Shadow, who was dressed in Native American garb. A bus soon arrived with children dancing and chanting through the paths of Pillar Cemetery. Begay stood next to Brien, words unnecessary.

Autumn also came to the ceremony with her aunt, Sister Francis, who deeply admired her mother's tombstone, now cleaned and highly polished. The new sitting bench was so beautiful and comfortable.

Brien approached them. "It seems so long ago when we first met here," kissing Autumn on her cheek. "Come with me. I want to show you everything that I've done to make Pillar Cemetery beautiful. She took his hand walking together on the new white stone pathways, weaving around the tombstones polished and shinning in the sunlight. She ran her fingers over the yellow daisy bushes and smelled the red and yellow roses.

"How utterly stunning. This graveyard has become fairytale beautiful," she said taken aback. They walked by the tall redwood fences and touched the lavender bushes like old friends.

"Look up at that pine tree. Meet my little friend Alpha," said Brien. "That mother owl has been watching us. I just love her.

When I've stayed overnight, I'd have conversations with her and she'd watch me and hoot," he said laughing. "I'd like to come here and watch her and sleep with you."

"Oh, baby, you can count on it," he said, hugging her.

He didn't tell her that one night in the graveyard while in his sleeping bag he had been unable to stop from crying over the murders of the Wongs and the Manchester twin boys. Suddenly he had heard the flapping of wings. When he opened his eyes, he saw the mother owl on the tombstone next to him hooting and hooting until he closed his eyes entering into a deep peaceful sleep. That's why he had grown to love the mother owl so much.

Chapter 18

Begay asked Carey to attend a computer technology convention on a Saturday morning. Carey, full of confidence, dressed in a light grey suit and sat next to a young, attractive brunette, pen in hand to take notes.

"How are you?" she asked pleasantly. "My name is Maureen and yours?"

"Carey, a pleasure to meet you," he said, watching her take notes. He didn't bother due to his extraordinary memory.

"You don't need to take notes?" she asked.

"I forgot my notepad. Was running late," he replied, unwilling to tell her he had no need.

"Here, take this one," she said pulling a notepad out of her briefcase.

"All of this is so new for me," he said, though it wasn't.

"I come to these conventions all the time," she said.

"Do you come for work?"

"Yes, I'm an accountant and it's important to keep up with the latest."

"How about lunch?" he asked, shocked how much he was feeling at ease, something he had never experienced with women before. For the rest of the day, the two enjoyed each other's company.

In the following weeks, they'd meet for lunch, and she'd share stories about her family.

"By the way," she said, "You never told me what you do for a living." The dreaded question had come. He could lie or tell her the truth.

"I'm a police officer detective," he said holding his breath.

"How exciting," she stated. "Is your work very difficult?"

"I'd say very challenging."

"Can you explain what you mean by challenging?" Carey wondered how forthright he could be or just outright tell her.

"I specialize on difficult murder cases," taking a deep breath watching for her reaction."

"I've read lots of murder mysteries."

He couldn't stop from laughing. "I assure you my work on murder cases is quite different."

He told her about Rambo, his bunny. "I can't believe it, but I have a rabbit too and her name is Peaches."

Begay noticed that Carey was going through a personal transition, not only physically but personality-wise, too. He was eager to leave work at five most nights to be with his girlfriend.

No one called him "The Kid" anymore. Rowling wanted to ask who his new flame was but thought better of it. Everyone was dying of curiosity. Then the day came when Carey showed everyone a photo of his new girlfriend: 5'8" with golden brown, wavy hair past her shoulders, hazel eyes and a charming smile. *Shock* was a tiny word for their reaction.

Brien wanted Autumn to be in his life as his wife fearing she did not have the same feelings for him. Finally, he asked Autumn to come to his house. Leonardo tried to calm him.

"I know she loves you."

"How do you know?"

"Because I'm old and very wise," he said very sincerely.

The doorbell rang and Leonardo left.

"Let's walk together in my gardens. I have an area just for fruit, vegetables and herbs." She noticed a large doggy door.

"Do you have a dog?"

"Was going to get one but the dog I wanted was adopted by someone else." The truth was he hoped it would be for Winston someday.

For a while they walked to another garden area filled with jasmine and honeysuckle and toward the end of his acreage stood a regal redwood tree of long years. "Your land and gardens are so breathtaking." He put his arm tight around her.

"I love you. I want you in my life forever. I want you to be my wife. Will you marry me?"

"I will. I will," she said weeping as he put a 14K Montana yellow gold sapphire on her finger.

Chapter 19

The Roosevelt room filled up quickly for the celebration dinner honoring Police Chief Begay's successful department transformation and from solving the infamous murder cases of Mr. and Mrs. Wong and Judge Manchester's twin nine-year-old boys. Alonzo had been put in San Quentin for life, that is if he lived long enough. Barbieri was serving a long sentence in a federal prison.

The front table was decorated with a long linen tablecloths and with yellow, white, and red roses in tall, crystal vases. Ex-mayor Reynolds of San Francisco, now the new governor, sat beside Chief Finn Begay and his wife, and Begay's assistant Chief Rowling.

The prosecution team sat next to them including Howard Daley, Brien Hogan, Claire Hobbins, and police detective Carey

Jones. All of the police officers looked smart in their police dress uniforms, enjoying the moment with bouncing gaiety.

Light classical music played in the background until Carey rose from the table, moving quickly to the podium.

"It gives me great pleasure to be your master of ceremonies. A real shocker, don't you think?" Everyone laughed. Carey, once called "The Kid," was no longer skinnier than a broomstick with stuttering speech. His hair was now brown and thick, and his body, quarterback fit. He was rather handsome and no longer wore glasses. His confident baritone voice echoed throughout the packed room.

When it was his turn to speak, Chief Begay spoke about the skill and work of all of his officers in solving the murders. Returning to his chair, he drew in a deep breath. God almighty, he had achieved the seemingly impossible, and it was a new day for his police force to keep on being the best of the best.

In the back of the room sat Shadow remembering their father's exhortation: "Don't keep your feet stuck in the mud less you miss the glory of the sunshine." Shadow watched his brother speak, recalling how, as innocent children, they played with sticks and stones. The next day everyone assembled in the Brady room feeling more at ease. Begay and Rowling came in chatting companionably.

"Today is special," said Begay. "I have a long list of promotions and wage increases." Everyone stood clapping. Begay's tough demeanor had changed. In fact, he looked downright beautiful. In a month's time domestic violence among the officers no longer existed. Wives were provided physical safety including financial help if needed. It was rumored that an officer early one morning had beat his wife so badly she ended up in the E.R. and so did the officer thanks to Begay who fired him in his hospital bed and later jailed him.

Chapter 20

Five days before Brien and Autumn's wedding, Begay was in charge of providing security for the wedding and had been asked to sweep the area. He entered the cemetery with two of his police officers and the head of Hastings Security, the best in the state of California.

"Go through every inch of this place and tell me what needs to be done," Begay said to Rust, head of security, a young, no-nonsense man. Begay admired the graveyard's transformation. Trees had been planted and birds had begun to nest. All of the tombstones had been transformed and no longer broken. Pleasant pathways filled the spaces around them. Begay stopped ten feet from the new marble mausoleum where a hawk was perched on top starring at him. He drew back quickly. He had learned from the old ones not to approach such a bird, moving from it respectfully and avoiding the temptation to glance at it quickly.

Begay was astonished that Brien had spent millions to beautify the old graveyard and couldn't believe this was where Brien and Autumn wanted to be married. Everyone involved with the party would be paid in hundred-dollar bills for their service. Begay refused to take any money, eventually finding out it had been given to his wife for his kids' lifelong education.

On the couple's wedding day, Brien stood on the top of the hill dressed in a light grey-blue suit and gold tie. He moved restlessly from foot to foot watching the white limousines parking and the people being escorted to their chairs decorated with white, flowing ribbons. Guards dressed in smart white tuxes watched everyone entering the wedding ceremony.

Brien loved Autumn more than anyone in his life. It seemed as if it had taken years for this glorious day to arrive. Children sat by their parents excited by the unknown. Begay sat in front with his wife and kids. Brien's boss, Howard Daley, and his assistant, Claire Hobbins, with her husband and children arrived filled with happiness. Everyone had stood when the wedding march of "Here Comes the Bride" had begun. Autumn took the hand of her father walking through an arch of white roses woven together in the shape of hearts. She wore a long, white satin gown with Irish lace that reached below her hips. Winston, in good behavior, wore a bright white bow and was under Bonnie's care.

Noah, Brien's best man, stood beside Brien whispering, "Hang in there, buddy," aware that Brien needed to hold it together. Autumn stood by the priest drawing in deep breaths.

Father Ignatius smiled. "You have agreed to hold dear your sacred bond of marriage. Now is the time to say your vows intended to guide you in the years to come. Brien, please pronounce your vows."

"I promise to be your husband and from this day forward to share my life with you in health and sickness, and with love, faith and joy for all the days of my life."

"Autumn you may pronounce your vows."

"I promise to be your wife and from this day forward to share my life with you in health and sickness and with love, and with faith and joy for all the days of my life."

"I now pronounce you husband and wife. You may kiss the bride." As they did everyone clapped and Winston barked loud and long.

It felt like a dream come true. The once LONELY GRAVEYARD and with all the polished tombstones had become breathtakingly beautiful with young bushes, flowers, and new trees amidst ornate iron rod fences and a secure gate. Sister Francis sat with another nun alongside everyone her face creased with smiles.

Autumn couldn't believe she had become Brien's wife and married in this old, now glorious, graveyard. In the distance a band began playing. Children played hide and seek around the tombstones falling over with laughter.

Begay leaned against the marble mausoleum, the sun filling it with shimmering light. It seemed alive and almost human, tall, elegant and even watchful. All the tombstones had long histories, filled with the mystery of lives once lived. Begay whispered a prayer, "Oh, Great Spirit, I hear your voice in the wind, whose breath gives life to all the world." He remembered the old ones speaking of what could not be understood, rubbing his hands with care and respect on the mausoleum's warm marble, knowing he would often return in conversation. Doves flew to the top of the mausoleum and began to coo in song. Begay watched the children excited in play and the great birds high in the branch trees nesting on the first day of spring. He took note of young Carey dancing with his sweet girlfriend, an Irish lassie from Shannon, Ireland.

Brien walked to the tables filled with Mexican, Italian, and American food where his wife was waiting for him.

"We can dance now or later," she said.

He kissed her. "Let's dance now."

Brien held Autumn tightly. He smiled to himself, having put in a white marble tombstone only for himself and dared not mention that to a soul, glancing at the nuns enjoying, from what he could see, a fine meal.

Begay smiled watching the children in play. "No more lonely graveyard. No. No. No," they sang.

When Begay returned to his car, his private number rang. "I want to thank you for your generous donation honoring your parents and thus continuing after so many years," said Abbot Ambrose of the Saint Francis Monastery.

"Thank you. How are things coming along in your monastery?"

"Miraculously."

"How so?"

"Several months ago, a man arrived wanting to use one of our cottages. He offered us so much money, that I needed to refuse. Instead, he said he was a contractor and would renovate all the buildings and restore our gardens to their former glory. He comes from time to time, having rebuilt the cottage he stays in, and he has even built a large family cottage.

"He pays the gardeners and gives us money every month to keep up our monastery. Must say he loves to drive me at top speed around in his white Lambo," he said, unsure of how to pronounce the name.

Begay's heart began pounding. "Would that be a Lamborghini?"

"That's right. He always brings his large Anatolian who shadows him everywhere. It's been such a miracle."

"I agree.

"Let us keep in touch."

It took a while for Begay to process his emotions. His former friend had found a new life and, as the abbot would say, redemption.

Begay watched the children play and the people dance. Even the mother owl in the distance appeared in a cheery mood. The once dilapidated mausoleum looked even more majestic with the sun blessing it with warmth. Children ran to Begay holding hands and forming a wide circle around him, singing, "Oh, Happy Graveyard. Oh, Happy Graveyard. " Begay wiped his eyes.

Acknowledgments

I deeply appreciate my talented team; with Catherine Lyon, my
marketing specialist, and Deborah Perdue,
my talented book designer, and editors Wendy Scheuring and
Joni Wilson for making this book special.

About the Author

Elizabeth Upton is the author of a number of other fiction and nonfiction titles. She received a BA from Syracuse University and an MA from Chapman University in Psychology. For over thirty years she has served as a family counselor, social worker and probation officer working with troubled teens and abused children. Elizabeth is married and lives in
Santa Barbara, California.